Gecko
and
Mosquito

For Anna

© 2007 Melissa DeSica

All rights reserved. No part of this book may be reproduced in any form or by any electronic or mechanical means, including information retrieval systems, without prior written permission from the publisher, except for brief passages quoted in reviews.

ISBN 978-0-9790647-6-0

Library of Congress Control Number: 2007925994

Design
Leo Gonzalez
Maggie Fujino

WATERMARK PUBLISHING
1088 Bishop Street, Suite 310
Honolulu, HI 96813
TELEPHONE: Toll-free 1-866-900-BOOK
WEB SITE: www.bookshawaii.net
EMAIL: sales@bookshawaii.net

Printed in Korea

Gecko and Mosquito

Melissa DeSica

Gecko declared himself king of the *hale*.
"I'm the head honcho, the house top tamale!"
To the bugs Gecko shouted, "I'm bigger than you!
Who's stronger? Who's smarter? *Moʻo*, that's who!"

He greedily gorged on bugs slow and weak,
He tricked the *lōlō*, scared the timid and meek.
But to one little bug he just could not get close,
It was tasty Mosquito he wanted the most.

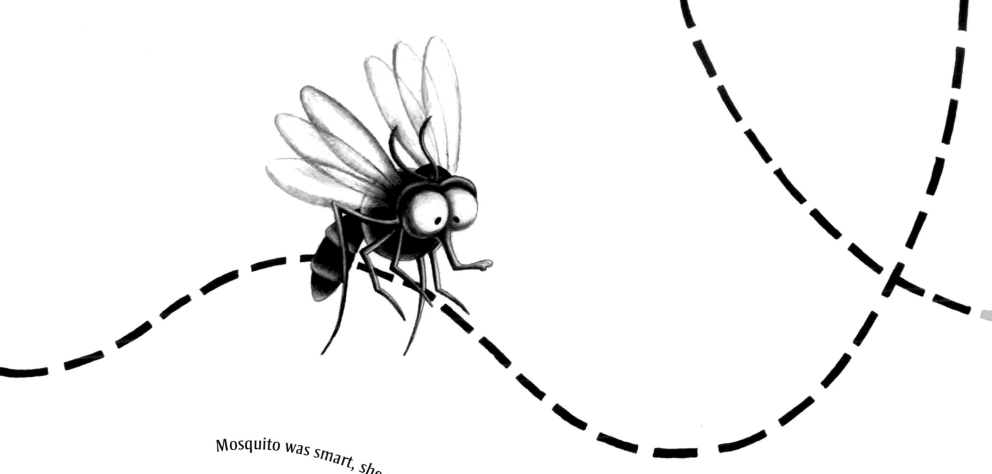

Mosquito was smart, she was fast, she was sly. That is what, in Hawaiian, we call akamai.

She was angry with Gecko, the games he would play, scaring those bugs in his sinister way.

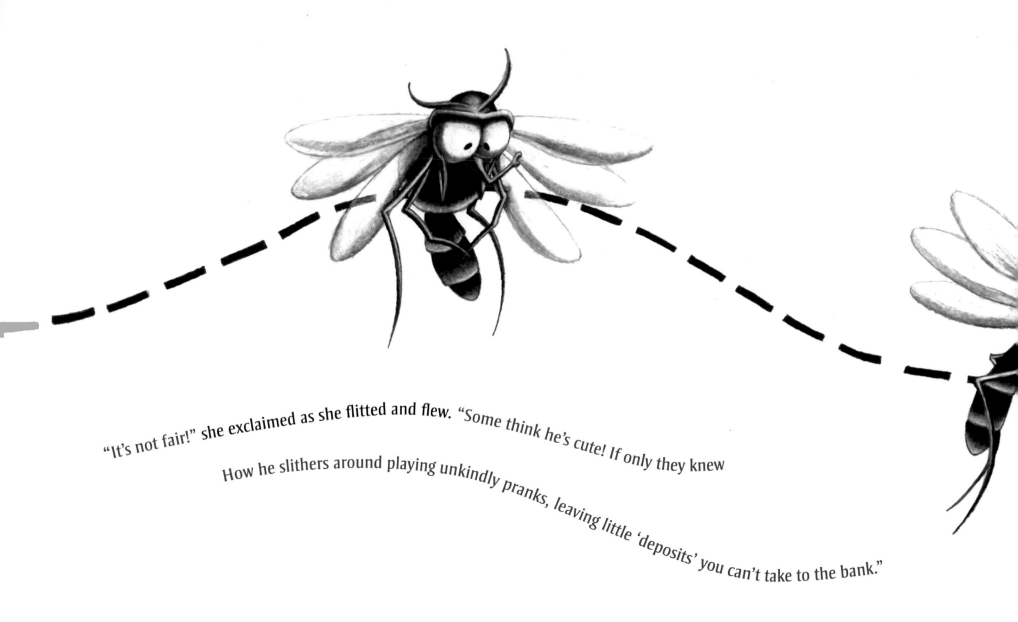

"It's not fair!" she exclaimed as she flitted and flew. "Some think he's cute! If only they knew

How he slithers around playing unkindly pranks, leaving little 'deposits' you can't take to the bank."

"But when I take a nibble on somebody's arm,

They scream and they holler and sound the alarm.

They slap me and smack me, squirt bug spray and curse me,

Though I try to explain that I'm really just thirsty.

"I'd love friends to play with, to accept who I am,

Who won't try to squash me as fast as they can.

But the bugs are being eaten, people shoo me away,

I don't feel the *aloha*, try as I may."

One morning she paused by the edge of the sink,

The water was soothing, a good place to think.

But she failed to notice that Gecko was near,

And he closed in behind, creeping up from the rear.

Then he slithered as fast as a gecko can go,

Without any warning, not even "hello."

"Mosquito!" he hollered. "My breakfast buffet!"

He was almost upon her, but she flitted away!

Her tiny heart pounded, she was scared, she was shaky,
So she stopped, soothed her nerves, took a drink on a *keiki*.
But Gecko still wanted Mosquito for *kaukau*,
His eyes big as lychees, his breath so *pilau*!

As he crept up behind her, Mosquito took flight,
The *keiki* saw Gecko and hollered in fright.
Mosquito flew panting from the arm of her host,
A narrow escape that was ever so close!

So she went to see Cock-a-roach, sweet and serene,

Chewing a page in a slick magazine.

"Howzit!" she said, "Wanna come out and play?

And help me forget about G. for the day?"

But Gecko sure hadn't forgotten the skeeter,

He was dreaming up new ways to catch her and eat her.

"My 'ōpū is rumbling, I can feel it grow thinner,

So I'll make me a bugwich and have it for dinner!"

"Run, Cock-a-roach!" cried Mosquito in warning,

"That gecko's been hunting me most of the morning!"

But before her new playmate could flee from the lizard,

He found himself swallowed, way down to its gizzard!

"This cannot continue!" cried angry Mosquito,

"Soon we'll all dwell in the '*ōpū* of *Mo'o*!

I must find a good way to stop him somehow,

And help save my bug friends from being *kaukau*!"

So all afternoon she racked her bug brain,

For just the right plan to make Gecko refrain

From serving her friends as his Catch of the Day.

Why, he'd never imagine the trick *she* would play!

Away 'round the house for an hour she flew, getting string, scissors, paper, paint, rocks and some glue.

She laid out her blueprints and sketched out a map, then went right to work to assemble her trap.

MosQUI-TWO

And when she was *pau*, to the window she flew
Where she baited her trap, a sculpture in blue.
"He's not going to get any more of my friends.
This trick will assure he *can't* do it again."

"I'm tired" she yawned, loud enough for all ears.
   "This sill does look cozy, I think I'll rest here."
She yawned a bit more, then ducked out of sight.
   She hid in a flowerpot and sat very tight.

When Gecko heard yawning, he could not resist,
His big chance to catch her just couldn't be missed.
As he leapt on "Mosqui-Two" his body was shaking,
The juiciest bug, finally his for the taking!

But something was wrong, he knew as he swallowed.
Where was the bug juice, and the flavor that followed?
This mosquito, he thought, was odd to the taste.
Why did it remind him of library paste?

He kicked with his legs, tried to push himself upward;
He begged for *kōkua*, but not one creature answered.
Any bug who could possibly come to his aid,
He'd already eaten on his nocturnal raid.

Then out popped Mosquito from her small hiding place.

She flew up to Gecko, got right in his face.

"*Mahalo* for eating my new body double,

I hope my surprise hasn't caused too much trouble!

And how is that *'ōpū*, that ripe swollen belly,

All heavy and bloated like a big bag of jelly?"

Gecko, he glowered, there was nothing to do,

Except squirm and moan softly, and feel like a fool.

"All right! I relent, I give up, I give in!

No more snacking on skeeters! Are you happy? You win!

But how can you laugh? Do you think this is funny?

This taste in my mouth, these rocks in my tummy?"

"Did *you* think it was funny to swallow my friends?

Now there's no way you can do it again.

Be grateful that I'm not as heartless as you!

I've no stomach for bites of *pilau* lizard stew.

"However, you've left a bad taste in *my* mouth.

This *hale* is not a hospitable house.

So I'll find a new one, a place to call home,

With lots of bug pals where I won't be alone."

And with that the mosquito grabbed all of her stuff,

Zipped right out the window and left in a huff.

When she found a new home, she had just one thing to ask:

"Are you sure there are no geckos here?"

Our brave little 'Squito was happy at last.

HAWAIIAN WORDS

Akamai (ah-ka-my)—Smart

Aloha (ah-loh-ha)—Hello, goodbye, love

Hale (ha-lay)—House

Kaukau (cow-cow)—Food (pidgin)

Keiki (kay-kee)—Child

Kōkua (koh-koo-ah)—Help, support

Lōlō (loh-loh)—Silly, stupid

Mahalo (ma-ha-loh)—Thank you

Moʻo (moh-oh)—Lizard

ʻŌpū (oh-poo)—Belly

Pau (pow)—Finished

Pilau (pee-lau)—Stinky